SAY
CHEESE!

Gareth Owen

Illustrated by Tim Archbold

YOUNG CORGI BOOKS

Amy put the camera on the table and pressed the blue button. Then she started to count.

"Hurry," said Grandad.

Amy started to count.

"ONE – TWO –
THREE – FOUR –"

She ran as quickly as she could. Everybody was still saying 'cheese'.

"Cheese!" shouted Amy. She tripped over the carpet and bumped into David. He fell on to the sideboard and the flowers and water fell all over Brillo's head.

FLASH!

Chapter One

It was Amy's birthday. When she came downstairs, everybody sang 'Happy Birthday, dear Amy'.

Her dad handed her a parcel. "Here's your special birthday present, Amy."

Amy looked at the parcel. "I wonder what it is," she said.

"Open it," said Mum.

Amy unwrapped the parcel

excitedly. She took out a small box. It was a camera. Her very own camera. Her dad showed her how to use it.

"You press this red button here."

"This one," said Amy. She put her finger on the button.

"Not yet!" said her dad.

But it was too late. Amy pressed the button.

FLASH!

"Yippee!" shouted Amy. "My first photograph. I bet it will be brilliant."

"Well, maybe," said her dad.

"I've got an idea," said her mum. "Why don't you take a photo of all of us?"

"Brilliant," said Amy. "All line up then."

"Make sure you've got us all in and that we're not moving this time," said her dad.

Amy looked through the viewfinder.

"Brilliant," she said.

"Then everybody say 'Cheese'," said Grandad.

"Cheese?" said Amy. "Why 'cheese'?"

"If you say 'cheese'," said Grandad, "you have to smile."

They all lined up. Mum, Dad, her brother David, Grandad. Even Brillo, the dog.

Amy looked through the viewfinder.

Her mum said, "What about you, Amy? Don't you want to be in the photo as well?"

"Me?" said Amy. "How can I be in the photo? I'm here. I'm taking the picture."

"There's a blue button on the top," explained her mother. "If you press that and count to five, you can walk over and be in the picture as well."

11

"I know, I know," said Amy.

She put the camera on the table and pressed the blue button. Then she started to count.

"Hurry," said Grandad.

Amy started to count.

"ONE – TWO – THREE – FOUR –"

She ran as quickly as she could. Everybody was still saying 'cheese'.

"CHEESE!" shouted Amy. She tripped over the carpet and bumped into David. He fell on to the sideboard and the flowers and water fell all over Brillo's head.

FLASH!

Amy picked herself up and faced the camera. "Cheese," she shouted again.

Brillo ran out of the room with daisies on his head. Amy smiled her biggest smile. She was really pleased.

Her father tried to explain that the camera had gone off too soon.

But Amy didn't listen. She couldn't wait to get to school and show her new camera to Mrs Clark, her teacher, and all her class.

Chapter Two

Mrs Clark stood in front of the class.
She was holding a silver cup.

"Don't forget, Class Three, about
the photo competition," she said. "The
pupil who takes the best photographs
will win this cup and ten pounds."

Amy put her hand up. "Miss, Miss."

"What is it, Amy?"

Amy held up her new camera.
"Miss, I've got a new camera. I've
already taken two pictures."

"Two pictures! My goodness, Amy. Were they good ones?"

"Brilliant," said Amy proudly.

Tommy Tubbs laughed. "You couldn't take a good photo with that little camera."

"Oh yes, you can," said Amy.

"No, you can't. You need a big camera like mine," said Tommy Tubbs. "I bet mine cost a lot more than that stupid little thing."

"You wait and see," said Amy.

Tommy Tubbs laughed again. "Yes, wait and see how terrible they are."

"Now then, Tommy," said Mrs Clark. "I'm sure Amy's camera will take very good photographs."

Amy had an idea. It was sure to win the prize. She put her hand up again. "Mrs Clark, can I take a photo of everybody in the class?"

"What a good idea," said Mrs Clark. She looked at Amy's camera. "It's got a blue button. That means you can be in the picture as well, Amy."

"I know, I know," said Amy.

All the class lined up, facing Amy. They left an empty chair in the middle for her. Mrs Clark stood at the back. Amy looked through the viewfinder.

"Say cheese, everybody," shouted Amy.

All the class shouted 'Cheese' at the tops of their voices, and smiled.

Amy was determined to get it right this time. She would walk carefully.

She wouldn't trip over anything.
"Ready? Here we go."

She pressed the blue button and
walked carefully towards her chair,
counting, "ONE – TWO –
THREE –"

There was a buzzing noise. A wasp
droned in through the open window.

"Wasp, wasp!"
screamed Tommy Tubbs,
flapping his hands.

The class jumped up. Their smiles
disappeared.

"Keep calm, everybody," said Mrs
Clark.

But everyone ran shouting in
different directions. They crashed into
one another. The chairs were turned
over. Tommy Tubbs ran to the
cupboard and locked himself in.

"Nothing to be frightened
of," shouted Mrs Clark.
"It's only a wasp."

The wasp landed in
her hair.

"Oh, no!" screamed Mrs Clark. "Go away, you horrible wasp." She flapped at it with the register.

Amy didn't notice any of this. She carried on counting and walked to her place. She sat down and looked at the camera.

"Cheese!" she said, and smiled.

FLASH!

Amy was pleased. She had managed to reach her place. That was three good pictures. She was even more sure now that she would win the first prize.

Chapter Three

In the afternoon, Amy's class went swimming. She took her camera along. She wanted to take a photograph of Tina, her best friend. Tina was wearing her new bathing costume.

"Tina, stand by the edge of the pool," Amy told her. She looked through her camera.

Somebody snatched the camera out of her hand. It was Tommy Tubbs. He still had his school uniform on. His mother didn't like him to go swimming in case he caught a cold.

"Give me that," he said. "I'll show you how to take proper photographs." He looked through the viewfinder. "That's no good. You can't see her head and feet. You have to get her all in the picture. Here, you take a photograph of me, and I'll tell you what to do." He handed the camera to Amy and went and stood next to Tina. "Am I all in?" he asked.

Amy looked through the viewfinder.

She could hardly see Tina. "I can't
get you both in," she said.

"Never mind about Tina," said
Tommy. "I'm the one you want." He
pushed Tina out of the way and took
a step back. "Have you got me all in
now?"

"No," said Amy.

Tommy took another step

backwards. "Is that better?"

"Further back," shouted Amy.

Tommy stepped backwards again.
He was right on the edge of the pool.

Tina said, "Be careful, Tommy."

"Don't tell me what to do," said
Tommy. "What do girls know about
taking photographs?" He combed his
hair. "Have you got me all in now?"

"Not quite," said Amy.

Tommy stepped back once more.
His foot was over the edge. He
swayed backwards.

"Perfect," said Amy.

Tommy swayed forwards. His
hands waved in the air.

"Keep still please," said Amy.

"Say "cheese'," said Tina.

"OOOOOOOOOOOOOOH!"
screamed Tommy.

FLASH! went the camera.

SPLASH went Tommy.

Tommy spluttered in the water.

"Now you're all in," said Tina and
Amy. "All in the water."

Chapter Four

Amy walked back to school. She had
taken eleven photographs now. Some
of the best were of...
Mrs Sweet, the
lollipop lady...

Mr
Phillips walking his
dog...

Mrs Jones, the headteacher, taking P.E....

And her dad at the zoo.

Next Saturday was the day of the competition. She had one photo left in the camera. She wanted this one to be the best of all – the one that would be certain to win the first prize. What would it be? She stood in front of the school steps looking up. On the wall was a big poster. It said:

SATURDAY

ST MARY'S SCHOOL GRAND FUND RAISING
☆ **RAFFLE** ☆

PHOTOGRAPH COMPETITION

RAISE MONEY FOR THE SPORTS HALL

Then an idea came to her. I know what I'll do, thought Amy. I'll take a picture of myself standing next to the poster. She was sure nobody else would have thought of that.

29

This time she wanted to be sure to get it right. She put the camera on the wall, pointing it at the poster. She left a little space for herself. Perfect! Now then, Amy, she said to herself, press the button carefully. Count to five. Walk up to the poster. Face the camera, say 'Cheese' and Bingo! It would be perfect.

She was ready. She pressed the button. The camera began to tick.

"ONE – TWO — "

She walked up to the poster. Three, four. She turned. And five!

"CHEESE," she said in a loud voice. Just as she spoke, a man ran across in front of her.

FLASH!

Her best picture would be ruined.

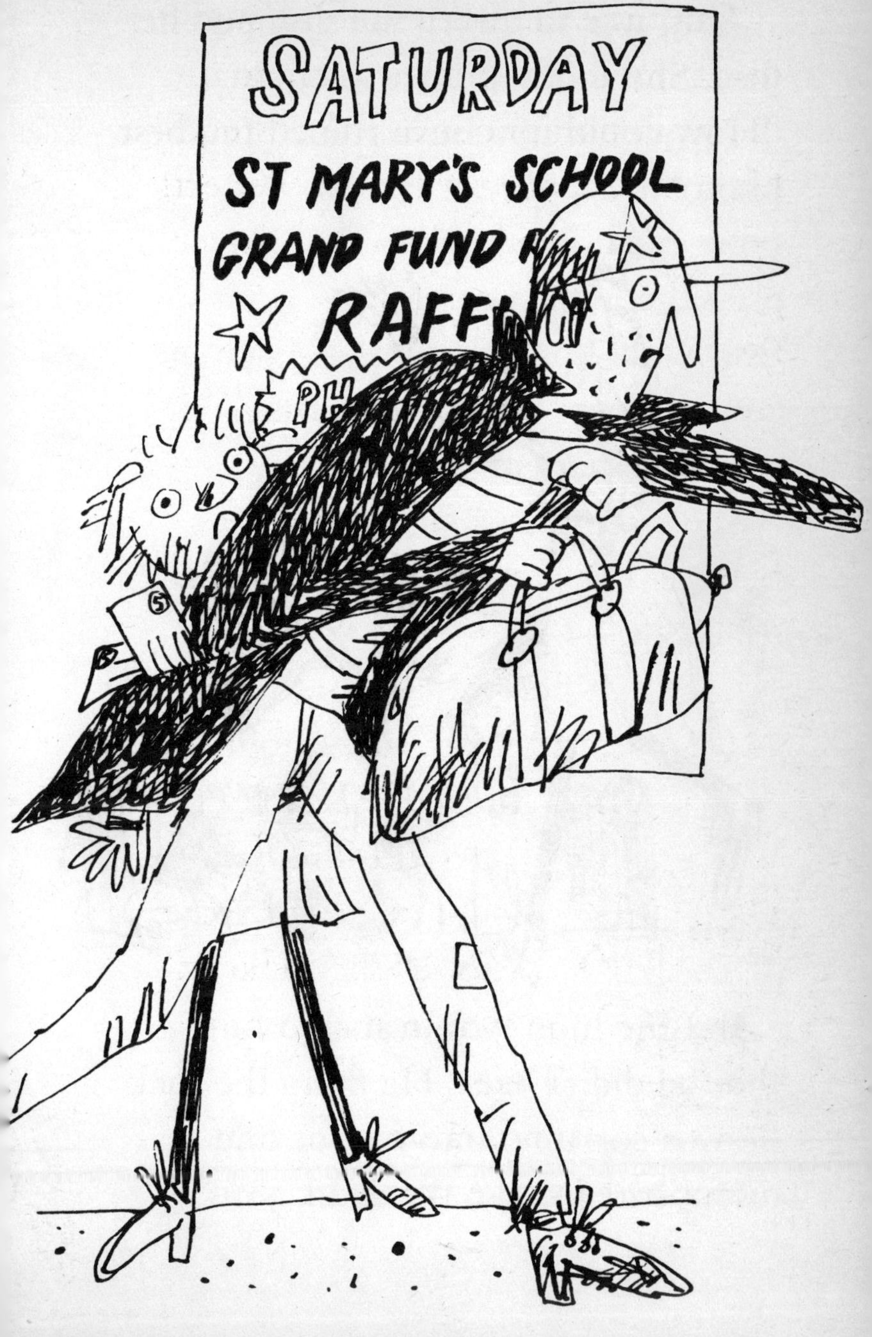
SATURDAY
ST MARY'S SCHOOL
GRAND FUND
RAFF
PH

Amy was so angry she stamped her foot. She shouted after the man. "How could you have ruined my best photo!"

But the man was in such a hurry that he didn't hear. He flung the sack he was carrying into his car and disappeared down the road.

Amy picked up her camera. Never mind, she thought. I've got eleven brilliant pictures. That will be enough to win the competition.

She ran home as fast as she could. Her father would take the photographs to be developed in time for the competition. As she ran, she thought about what she would buy with the ten pounds prize.

Chapter Five

It was the day of the competition. In
the school hall, the children were
pinning their photographs on the wall.

One by one the people began to
arrive. Mrs Clark, Mrs Sweet the
lollipop lady, Mrs Phillips, Tommy
Tubbs and his mother, Amy's mum,
David, Grandad – and even Brillo.

Amy ran over to her mum. "Where's Dad?"

"Isn't he here?" said Amy's mum. "He left early in the car. He was going to the chemists to pick up your photos. He must be here somewhere."

Amy looked around but she couldn't see her dad anywhere. Mrs Clark was walking round, speaking to all the children. Tommy Tubbs's photographs were all neatly mounted and pinned up on the wall. He stood proudly in front of his display.

"Well done, Tommy," said Mrs Clark.

Tommy's mother patted his head. "Aren't you a clever boy," she said.

Tommy smiled and combed his hair. "Yes, I suppose I am. The important thing in photographs is to get the legs and the head in."

Mrs Clark moved on to the next child. "Such a clever boy," said Tommy's mum and kissed him on the cheek.

When Mrs Clark reached the last display, she found Amy standing in front of an empty space.

"Amy dear, where are your photos?"

"I don't know," said Amy.

"Don't know? What do you mean, you don't know?"

"They haven't got here yet."

Mrs Clark looked at her watch. "Haven't got here?" she said. "But Amy, it's ten to eleven. The judging begins in ten minutes. If you don't pin up your photos soon, it will be too late. Where are they?"

"Dad's supposed to be bringing them from the chemist's shop, but he hasn't got here yet," Amy said.

Mrs Clark frowned. "Well, I hope he's quick. The Mayor will be here any minute."

"Dad will be here soon, won't he?" said Amy.

"I hope so," said Mrs Clark.

Amy hoped so, too. Where was her dad? She heard a car driving up. Perhaps that was him? She ran to the front door. She looked up and down the street. There was no sign of him. A huge car drew up. It was the Lord Mayor.

Amy ran back to the hall. Tommy Tubbs was standing in front of Amy's space. He said, "Look, Amy's photos are so terrible she's ashamed to put them up."

"They're not terrible," said Amy.

"Where are they then?" said Tommy with a smirk.

"My dad's bringing them."

Tommy laughed. "That's what you say. I bet they came out so bad that he threw them in the rubbish bin."

"He did not," said Amy.

"Yes, he did, because I saw him," said Tommy. He walked away laughing.

Amy felt like crying. Where was her dad?

Her mum came over. "Don't worry, dear," she said. "He'll be here soon. He won't let you down."

The clock on the wall said

two minutes to eleven.

The Mayor came into the hall with the headteacher. The headteacher rang a bell. Everybody went quiet.

"Ladies and gentlemen, parents, teachers and children. I'm very pleased to welcome you all to St Mary's School for our photographic competition. I'm very honoured that the Lord Mayor has agreed to be the judge."

The Mayor bowed and everybody clapped. The headteacher said, "I'm very pleased to tell you that we've managed to collect five hundred pounds towards the new Sports Hall."

Five hundred pounds! Everybody cheered even louder.

The Mayor laughed. "It's a lot of money, Headteacher. I hope you've got it safe somewhere."

"Oh, yes, it's quite safe," said the headteacher. "Locked up in my office with the silver cup."

Everybody laughed.

But Amy wasn't listening to all this. She was nearly in tears. Where was her dad? He'd promised her he'd be there. Had he really thrown her photos in the rubbish bin?

The headteacher said, "Well, all that remains is for the Mayor to go round to judge the photographs."

The Mayor and the headteacher walked round the hall. They looked carefully at all the photos. Tommy Tubbs was the first.

"Tell me, Tommy, what do you try to do when you take a photograph?"

Tommy smiled. "The important thing is to get all the legs and the head in."

"Quite right," said the Mayor. "Quite right."

"Such a clever boy," said Tommy's mum.

The Mayor moved on.

Mrs Clark came over to where Amy was hiding. "Amy, why aren't you standing by your photographs?"

Amy could hardly speak. "B..b.. because Dad hasn't brought them yet. Now it's too late. Perhaps they were so bad that he threw them away."

Just then the doors at the back of the
hall burst open. A man rushed in. His
hands and face were streaked with oil
and grease.

"Dad!" shouted Amy and ran over
to him.

"Sorry I'm late, Amy. The car broke down. I bet you thought I wasn't coming, didn't you?" He gave Amy a hug.

Amy shook her head. "Oh no, Dad, I knew you'd get here," she said.

The Mayor had nearly reached Amy's space.

Mrs Clark ran over to them. She snatched the photographs. "Quick, let me pin them up or it will be too late."

She pushed her way through all the people and began pinning up Amy's pictures as quickly as she could. She was just pinning up the very last photo when the Mayor said, "And whose are these pictures?"

"These are Amy's photos," said Mrs Clark.

Amy was helping her dad to wipe

the oil and grease off his face and
hands.

"Ah," said the Mayor. "Let me
see."

The Mayor and the headteacher
peered at the photographs. Suddenly
the strangest thing happened. The
Mayor's whole body began to shake
like a jelly. Then he made a sound
that sounded like a cough. The
cough became a chuckle. The
chuckle a giggle. the giggle a laugh
and the laugh a guffaw. Then the
headteacher began to laugh.
Everybody wondered what they
could be laughing at.

They gathered round Amy's pictures. Everybody was pointing and laughing. Amy looked up. What could they all be laughing at? She pushed her way through the crowd. And then she saw them. Her photographs. They had all come out wrong.

Amy felt so ashamed. The Mayor
couldn't stop laughing. He pointed.
"Oh, my goodness, look at that. Look
at that fat boy falling in the water. Ha
hahahahahaha."

Amy ran back to her mum. "My
pictures," she cried. "Everybody's
laughing at my pictures. They've all
come out wrong."

At last the Mayor managed to stop
laughing. He held up his hand for
silence. Amy hid her face in her dad's
side.

"Ladies and gentlemen," announced
the Mayor. "I've looked at everybody's

photographs and I think they're all wonderful and a credit to St Mary's School. But one group of photographs is by far the best. Now people say that there is a golden rule in photography and that is to 'always get the head and the legs in'.

Tommy Tubbs puffed out his chest and smirked. He pointed to himself. "I said that," he said.

"Such a clever boy," said his mum.

"However," went on the Mayor,

"rules are there to be broken, so I would like to award the cup to someone who has cheered us all up this afternoon. The winner is..."

He paused.

Tommy Tubbs's smile grew wider.

"The winner is AMY!"

Amy unburied her face. She thought she was hearing things.

"Who? Who did he say had won?"

"Amy," said her dad. "It's you. You've won!"

"Where is Amy?" asked the Mayor.

Her dad pushed Amy forward. Everybody clapped. The Mayor shook her hand.

"Headteacher," he said, "where's that cup so I can give it to Amy?"

But just then the headteacher came running across the hall. Her face was white. "Stop!" she cried. "Something terrible's happened!"

Chapter Six

"It's the cup!" said the headteacher.
"It's been stolen!"

"Stolen!" cried the Mayor.

"Stolen?" cried all the people.

"Yes," said the headteacher. "But it's not just the cup. It's worse than that."

"Worse?" said the Mayor.

"Yes," said the headteacher. "It's all the money. The five hundred pounds we collected for the Sports Hall.

That's been stolen as well."

Everybody began to talk at once.

"The cup stolen..."

"And the five hundred pounds.."

"Who could have stolen it?"

"Send for the police."

"Stop, thief."

Then one voice rang out above all the rest. It was Mrs Clark's voice. She had been looking at Amy's pictures. Suddenly she shouted, "There he is!"

"Where, where?" cried the headteacher. He looked about him.

"Over here," said Mrs Clark. "There he is. Look!"

She was pointing at the wall.

"Where?" said the headteacher. "What are you talking about? I can't see anybody."

Mrs Clark was pointing at one of Amy's photographs.

"There! There!" said Mrs Clark. "Can't you see? There's the cup."

"By Jove, you're right," said the Mayor.

Amy looked at the photo. It was the last one she had taken. She remembered the man who had spoiled the photo by running in front of her. It was the thief. She could see his face clearly.

The Mayor shook Amy by the hand. "Well done, Amy! With this picture, the police will soon catch the thief."

And it was true. Three weeks later, the man was caught. They showed Amy's photograph on the front page of the newspaper. It was even on the television. One day she even had her own photograph under the headline:

LOCAL GIRL HELPS TRAP THIEF

"It's a good photo," said Amy to her mum.

"Why's that?"

"It's got my legs and head in," said Amy.

But Amy didn't think it was as good as one of her photographs. After all, it didn't make you laugh at all.

Three days later, the Mayor came in person to give the prize and money to Amy. She felt very proud and put the cup on the table.

Before the Mayor left, he asked if he could take a photograph of himself with Amy with her camera. Of course Amy said yes.

It came out very well. One of Amy's best. The Mayor hasn't had his copy yet, but I'm sure he wouldn't mind you seeing it. Would he?

THE END